BOOKS for ME!

by
Sue Fliess

illustrated by
Mike Laughead

two lions

Thanks to librarians everywhere.

—S. F.

For Candace. Thank you for sharing
so many books and so many wonderful smiles.

—M. L.

Published by Two Lions, New York

www.apub.com

LCCN: 2014944828
ISBN-13: 9781477820360
ISBN-10: 1477820361

The illustrations are rendered in graphite, ink, and digital media.
Book design by Vera Soki

Printed in China
First Edition

BOOKS ARE AWESOME!

Reading's free. . . .

Let's go to the library!

Words are waiting
to be read—
new ideas to fill my head.

Lots of choices I can see.

Will I find some books for me?

Books on mittens,
broken chairs,
mice and moons
and puzzled bears.

Knights and castles,
kings and queens,
golden eggs
and magic beans.

Stacks of stories, wall to wall.

Listen as I read them all!

Books on jungles, lion kings,
monsters, creatures, wild things.

Books on pirates,
treasure hunts.

Who can read a
book just once?

Books on villains,

sneaky spies,

superheroes in disguise.

Folktales, fables,
old and new,

stories made-up,
stories true.

Books on battles, history.

"Dad, will you read these to me?"

Books on science,
books on math,
books for reading
in the bath!

Books on insects,
snails and slugs,
flying ants and
lightning bugs.

**Books on zombies,
phantom screams.**

Dad says, “No,
you’ll have bad dreams.”

Books on freight trains,
cars and trucks,

barnyard books
with pigs and ducks.

Mermaids, dragons
in my hands.
I escape to other lands.

Books on music,

books on art.

Reading books can make me smart!

Here's my favorite.
This one rhymes.
I have read it fifty times.

Time for checkout.

Can it be?

I have found some books for me!